W9-AUY-116

# The Curious Faun

by Raija Siekkinen
illustrations by Hannu Taina

Translated from the Finnish by Tim Steffa

Carolrhoda Books, Inc./Minneapolis

There once was a time when the woods were filled with fauns. They lived in caves lit by fireflies and warmed by flames that never went out.

The fauns led happy lives. They ate honey and drank from springs, and they knew nothing whatever of sorrow. All day long they played their flutes, and at night they told each other stories.

Every summer the fauns would gather in a forest clearing
for a faun feast. They sang and danced, and their merrymaking
was heard far and wide.

The farmers heard the music when they returned from their fields at sundown, weary with cares about the growth of their crops. The fishermen heard the music when they went out at daybreak to set their nets, burdened with worries about the next day's catch. Each person who heard the sounds of joy was troubled. Joy was unknown to humans, and it made them afraid.

So the people decided to find out what was making the strange noises. When they came upon the fauns and saw what a carefree life they led, the people were angry.

After all, why should fauns know nothing of sorrow, when they themselves knew nothing of joy? And their anger sharpened their hearing.

Now every night the people thrashed in their beds, disturbed by the sounds of flutes and curious whisperings. In the morning they grumbled that they were always tired because the fauns wouldn't let them sleep.

Together the people decided to do something about it.

A great faun hunt was organized. The people stormed
the forest armed with guns. They let loose their hounds and
fired at the fleeing fauns. The hounds drove the fauns deeper
and deeper into the woods.

From that day on fauns were shy. They told their tales in whispers, their flutes were rarely heard, and their feast was held during the darkest night of the year, lit only by the smallest of torches.

And from that day on the people slept well and did their day's work, harvesting crops and catching fish. Nothing disturbed their peace and quiet.

But then one day a young faun who was curious about the ways of humans decided to see the land of people for himself. This frightened the other fauns because they believed that people were wicked and foolish. But they gave him permission to go, for fauns find it almost impossible to refuse a request.

So off the little faun went. He climbed down the mountain and wound his way for many days through the green forest. He was joined by an old frog who, having seen all manner of things with his goggly eyes, considered himself wise enough to guide a faun in the land of people.

When the faun and the frog came at last to the land of
people, the faun gazed around in wonder.  Everything was
stony, gray, and cold.  No woodland murmur was heard here,
and there were no flowers to be seen.

The faun had often been told of the wickedness of people, so his first wish was this:

"I would like to see a wicked person."

"That is a wish fairly easily granted," said the frog.

The frog went away and returned almost at once and said, "I've found one. Here he comes now."

As the little faun watched, a man approached, kicking out angrily at anything that got in his way, and trying to step on the frog as he passed.

They followed the man to his house without his noticing a thing, for people had long since lost the ability to see fauns. Now they only saw what they knew was there.

The faun and the frog seated themselves on a windowsill and watched as the man stomped around the room. Then the man flung himself into a chair, muttering angrily to himself until at last he fell asleep. The faun and the frog moved closer to watch the wicked man's dreams. They saw that in his dreams he broke windows and trampled flowers.

"It's quite clear that he's feeling bad," said the faun. "I'll play a little for him. Perhaps that will help him forget his anger."

He took up his flute and played, and the melody entered the man's dreams. The faun played again the next night, and the next. Each morning the man awoke happier than the morning before. He wondered why he no longer awoke angry, and why his dreams had changed so much that one night he dreamed he had his very own frog to care for.

"How curious," the wicked man said to himself the next morning. "Somehow the world seems lovelier."

That day the man came home with a little puppy, and he said to it, "You are my friend and I will take care of you."

When the faun heard this, he said to the frog, "You must know nothing about people. I asked you to find a wicked person, but this man isn't wicked at all."

And off they went, leaving the man at home with his new puppy.

"What sort of person do you want to meet now?" asked the frog.

The faun had often been told of the foolishness of people, so his second wish was this:

"I would like to see a foolish person."

"That is a wish very easily granted," said the frog.

The frog went away and returned at once and said, "I found two of them for you."

And the faun followed the frog to a house that was filled with books. A man and a woman sat at a table, reading and mumbling to themselves.

All day long people came to them with questions. The two people explained all manner of things. If someone disagreed with them, one or the other would take down a book and look up a passage to prove they were right. The faun and the frog seated themselves on the edge of a book-shelf and watched. Finally the faun said to the frog, "These people can't be foolish. They seem to know everything."

"Just wait," said the frog.

The next visitor wanted to discuss fauns.

"There are no such things as fauns," the man and the woman said together. And they each took a book from a shelf and read long passages that stated that fauns did not exist.

"Well now," said the frog to the faun, "what do you say to that?"

"If that's what foolish people are like, I'd like to see a wise one now," said the faun.

"That is a very difficult wish to grant," said the frog. "It will take time. Wait for me here."

It was a long while before the frog returned.

The frog led the faun to a small house on the edge of the woods, where a man was strolling about the garden. Stopping from time to time, he looked at the stones and the grass and said to himself, "Why does that stone shine in the sunlight?" and "Why does that one blade of grass bend away from all the others? How curious. I must get to the bottom of this."

When the man went inside, the faun and the frog followed him into his house, which was filled with books.

"This doesn't look good," said the faun.

The man sat down at his table and began to write. Now and again he lifted his head and said, "Why does that branch keep tapping my window?" or "Why do I feel so happy and so sad at the same time?" or simply, "How curious. How very curious."

The faun and the frog perched on the mantel over the fireplace, watching the man thoughtfully.

"He doesn't sound very wise," the faun said. "He doesn't seem to know anything. But I like him anyway. How curious."

At this the wise person looked up.

"Who said 'HOW CURIOUS'?" he asked. And when he saw the faun and the frog, he smiled.

"A faun," he said. "And a frog. How very curious indeed."

"You must be mistaken," said the faun in sudden fright. "People can't see fauns."

"No, they can't," said the man. "But I can see you. It *is* very curious, isn't it?"

And the man and the faun began to talk. The man told the faun about the ways of humans. Then the faun told the man about the ways of fauns. And the frog sat on the mantel, blinking his goggly eyes and listening.

And so the little faun stayed with the man, and the frog returned to the land of fauns with word of what people were like. The more the fauns learned, the less frightened they were, and after a while the fauns came down from the mountain to the green valley below. They told their stories aloud once more, their flutes were heard once more, and once more they held their feasts during the brightest days of summer. They were no longer afraid of people. Instead they felt rather sorry for them, for they now understood that people's lives are filled with cares.

The wise person told the faun's tales throughout the land. And once again there were people in the world who believed that fauns existed. The more people learned about fauns, the less angry they were, and soon even the fauns' music disturbed them only a little.

The little faun remained in the land of people, curious to see what he might yet discover. Even now he might be somewhere nearby, quietly weaving his music into your thoughts, so that every now and then you may feel like saying HOW CURIOUS.

But the frog was old and weary and longed to rest.
He moved to a large pond deep in the woods. On summer
evenings you can hear him trilling in the twilight, happy
not to think of matters that don't really concern frogs.

This edition first published 1990 by Carolrhoda Books, Inc.
First published in Finland in 1988 by Otava Publishing
Company Ltd. under the title *Utelias Fauni*.
Text copyright © 1988 by Raija Siekkinen
Illustrations and typography copyright © 1988 by Hannu Taina
English-language translation copyright © 1988 by Tim Steffa
All English-language rights reserved by Carolrhoda Books, Inc.
Printed in Finland by Otava 1989 and bound in the United
States.

Library of Congress Cataloging-in-Publication Data

Siekkinen, Raija, 1953-
    The curious faun.

    Translation of: Utelias fauni.
    Summary: The people of the world, angry at the fauns
of the forest because of their carefree revels, chase
them up into the mountains; years later, one young faun
returns to spy on the people to find out why they have no
joy.
    [1. Satyrs (Greek mythology)—Fiction] I. Taina,
Hannu, ill. II. Title.
PZ7.S5764Cu   1990              [E]              89-972
ISBN 0-87614-379-6 (lib. bdg.)

1  2  3  4  5  6  7  8  9  10  99  98  97  96  95  94  93  92  91  90